IN THE CAPITAL OF SINDHU,* QUEEN DUHSHALA WAS ANXIOUSLY WAITING FOR THE RETURN OF HER HUSBAND, JAYADRATHA.

A CLOUD OF DUST IN THE DISTANCE! IT MUST BE MY HUSBAND RETURNING FROM HASTINAPURA.

YES, HE'S HERE! I CAN SEE HIS CHARIOT QUITE CLEARLY NOW.

* MODERN SINDH

I HOPE ALL IS WELL, MY LORD.

ALL IS WELL, DUHSHALA. IN FACT THINGS COULDN'T BE BETTER....

THE KAURAVAS, YOUR BROTHERS, HAVE FOUND A SUPREMELY CLEVER WAY OF HUMBLING YOUR COUSINS, THE PROUD PANDAVAS!

...HUMBLING THE PANDAVAS?

YES. THEY INVITED THE PANDAVAS TO PLAY A GAME OF DICE. THOUGH THE STAKE WAS HIGH, THE PANDAVAS COULDN'T REFUSE.

AND WHAT WAS THE STAKE?

THE LOSERS WOULD SURRENDER ALL RIGHTS TO THEIR KINGDOM AND GO INTO EXILE FOR THIRTEEN YEARS.

THE PANDAVAS FELL FOR THAT? DIDN'T THEY KNOW MY UNCLE, SHAKUNI, WOULD HELP MY BROTHERS TO WIN?

THE PANDAVAS ARE SIMPLETONS. AND YUDHISHTHIRA, THE ELDEST PANDAVA, ALLOWED SHAKUNI TO CAST THE DIE FOR DURYODHANA...

···NATURALLY, SHAKUNI WON THE GAME FOR DURYODHANA WITH HIS TRICKS. HA! HA! HA!

I FEEL A LITTLE SORRY FOR THE PANDAVAS. THEY HAVE TO PAY A HARD PRICE.

NO, DUHSHALA, IT'S A GOOD THING FOR US. YOUR BROTHERS WILL RULE AT HASTINAPURA AND WE STAND TO GAIN BY THAT.

MEANWHILE THE PANDAVAS — YUDHISHTHIRA, BHIMA, ARJUNA, NAKULA AND SAHADEVA — WITH THEIR WIFE, DRAUPADI, HAD REACHED THE KAMYAKA FOREST. LATER THEIR COUSIN, KRISHNA, AND OTHER RELATIVES AND FRIENDS VISITED THEM.

YUDHISHTHIRA, I AM FURIOUS AT THIS INJUSTICE. I WILL SLAY THE WICKED KAURAVAS AND INSTALL YOU AGAIN ON THE THRONE.

KRISHNA, HAVING PLAYED THE GAME I ACCEPT THE OUTCOME. BUT AFTER THIRTEEN YEARS WE WILL RETURN.

YOU ARE JUST AND NOBLE, YUDHISHTHIRA.

FAREWELL, MY FRIENDS. GOD WILLING, WE WILL MEET AGAIN IN HAPPIER TIMES.

FAREWELL!

FAREWELL!

THE PANDAVAS PASSED SEVERAL YEARS IN THE FOREST. ONE DAY THEY HAD GONE AWAY AS USUAL IN SEARCH OF GAME LEAVING DRAUPADI AT HOME.

THERE SEEM TO BE A LOT OF PEOPLE COMING THIS WAY. WHO COULD THEY BE?

OH! ONE OF THEM IS GALLOPING TOWARDS ME!

FAIR LADY, I HAVE BEEN SENT BY JAYADRATHA, KING OF SINDHU.

WE WERE PASSING BY WHEN HE SAW YOU. HE WISHES TO KNOW WHO YOU ARE.

I AM DRAUPADI, THE WIFE OF THE VALIANT PANDAVAS. MY HUSBANDS HAVE GONE OUT HUNTING. THEY WILL BE PLEASED TO HAVE YOUR KING AS THEIR GUEST.

WHEN THE INVITATION WAS CONVEYED TO JAYADRATHA—

SO IT IS DRAUPADI! AND SHE IS ALONE! I MUST CARRY HER AWAY BEFORE THE PANDAVAS RETURN.

DRAUPADI RECEIVED JAYADRATHA WITH DUE COURTESY.

O KING, ACCEPT WATER TO WASH YOUR FEET. I AM PLEASED TO DO THIS SERVICE FOR YOU ON BEHALF OF YUDHISHTHIRA.

AND I WILL BE PLEASED IF YOU WILL COME WITH ME AND BE MY QUEEN!

WHAT... WHAT DID YOU SAY?

WHY SHOULD YOU SUFFER WITH THE PANDAVAS? FORSAKE THEM. BE MY QUEEN AND LIVE IN COMFORT.

TO LAY HANDS ON ME IS TO INVITE THE WRATH OF ARJUNA AND BHIMA UPON YOURSELF. IT IS LIKE KICKING A SLEEPING LION. GO AT ONCE, IF YOU VALUE YOUR LIFE!

YOU CAN'T FRIGHTEN ME WITH SUCH THREATS!

WRETCH, DON'T DEFILE ME WITH YOUR TOUCH!

DISREGARDING HER ANGER, JAYADRATHA CARRIED HER TO HIS CHARIOT AND DROVE AWAY.

MEANWHILE THE PANDAVAS WERE RETURN-ING FROM THE HUNT—

THE BIRDS SEEM AGITATED. COULD SOME HOSTILE PEOPLE HAVE COME HERE? LET'S GO FASTER.

IT WAS NOT LONG BEFORE THE PANDAVAS DISCOVERED THAT DRAUPADI HAD BEEN ABDUCTED. IMMEDIATELY THEY SET OUT IN SEARCH OF HER.

LOOK, THERE ARE CHARIOT TRACKS HERE!

THEY MUST HAVE GONE THIS WAY! LET'S FOLLOW THEM!

THERE THEY ARE!

IN THE BATTLE THAT FOLLOWED, THE PANDAVAS SCATTERED JAYADRATHA'S ARMY.

JAYADRATHA FLED FOR HIS LIFE LEAVING DRAUPADI BEHIND.

DRAUPADI, GO BACK HOME WITH YUDHISHTHIRA. BHIMA AND I WILL PURSUE THAT SCOUNDREL.

FOR THE SAKE OF OUR COUSIN, DUHSHALA, DO NOT SLAY JAYADRA- THA, THOUGH HE IS SO WICKED!

JAYADRATHA WAS UNAWARE THAT BHIMA AND ARJUNA WERE ON HIS TRAIL.

I'VE HAD A CLEAR START. THE PANDAVAS CAN'T OVERTAKE ME NOW.

SUDDENLY—

MY HORSE! ARJUNA MUST BE AROUND SOMEWHERE!

JAYADRATHA SPRANG OUT OF HIS CHARIOT...

...AND STARTED TO RUN.

STOP, JAYADRATHA!

BHIMA SEIZED JAYADRATHA BY THE HAIR AND HELD HIM.

YOU COWARD! YOU DARE TO CARRY AWAY A LADY BY FORCE YET YOU RUN AWAY FROM A MAN!

BHIMA THEN THREW HIM TO THE GROUND WITH GREAT FORCE.

JAYADRATHA TRIED TO RUN AWAY, BUT BHIMA KICKED HIM HARD AND PRESSED HIM DOWN—

A WORM LIKE YOU SHOULD NOT BE ALLOWED TO LIVE.

BHIMA, DON'T KILL HIM. REMEMBER WHAT YUDHISHTHIRA TOLD US.

THEN BHIMA SHAVED JAYADRATHA'S HEAD.

IF YOU WISH TO LIVE YOU MUST PUBLICLY DECLARE THAT YOU ARE THE SLAVE OF THE PANDAVAS. WILL YOU DO SO?

YES.

THEN ARJUNA AND BHIMA BOUND JAYADRATHA IN CHAINS, THRUST HIM INTO THE CHARIOT...

...AND DROVE BACK HOME.

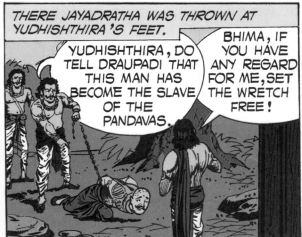

THERE JAYADRATHA WAS THROWN AT YUDHISHTHIRA'S FEET.

YUDHISHTHIRA, DO TELL DRAUPADI THAT THIS MAN HAS BECOME THE SLAVE OF THE PANDAVAS.

BHIMA, IF YOU HAVE ANY REGARD FOR ME, SET THE WRETCH FREE!

WHAT DO YOU SAY, DRAUPADI?

LET HIM GO! HE IS OUR SLAVE AND YOU HAVE SHAVED HIS HEAD. THAT IS ENOUGH FOR ME.

YOU ARE A FREE MAN NOW. NEVER SET YOUR HEART AGAIN ON EVIL DEEDS!

JAYADRATHA LEFT, BURNING WITH SHAME AND ANGER.

I WILL HAVE MY REVENGE....

HE WENT TO THE BANKS OF THE GANGA AND, IMPLORING THE PROTECTION OF LORD SHIVA, HE OBSERVED SEVERE PENANCES.

MANY YEARS PASSED BY. AT LAST LORD SHIVA APPEARED BEFORE HIM.

I AM PLEASED WITH YOU. ASK FOR A BOON.

LORD, I WANT TO BE ABLE TO DEFEAT ALL FIVE OF THE PANDAVAS IN BATTLE!

THAT IS NOT POSSIBLE. NO ONE CAN DEFEAT THE PANDAVAS.

HOWEVER, YOU WILL BE ABLE TO CHECK THE ADVANCE OF THE PANDAVAS ONCE. BUT EVEN SO YOU WON'T BE ABLE TO STOP ARJUNA.

JAYADRATHA RETURNED TO HIS KINGDOM. THEN HE BEGAN HIS LONG WAIT FOR REVENGE.

THE PANDAVAS HAVE COMPLETED THEIR PERIOD OF EXILE. WILL DURYODHANA RESTORE THEIR KINGDOM TO THEM? I HOPE NOT.

THEN ONE MORNING HE RECEIVED A MESSAGE FROM DURYODHANA.

"...I HAVE REFUSED TO GIVE THEM EVEN AN INCH OF LAND. THERE WILL BE WAR. COME TO MY HELP, JAYADRA-THA."

THIS IS THE NEWS I HAVE BEEN WAITING FOR — WAR, WAR WITH THE PANDAVAS!

THE GREAT WAR BETWEEN THE KAURAVAS AND THE PANDAVAS WAS FOUGHT ON THE FIELD OF KURUKSHETRA. WITH KRISHNA DRIVING HIS CHARIOT, ARJUNA AT-TACKED THE KAURAVA FORCES WITH LIGHTNING SPEED. ON THE TENTH DAY OF THE BATTLE, BHISHMA, THE COMMANDER OF THE KAURAVA FORCES, WAS MORTALLY WOUNDED BY ARJUNA'S ARROW.

DRONA TOOK HIS PLACE AS COMMANDER, BUT THE KAURAVAS CONTINUED TO LOSE HEAVILY. THREE DAYS LATER —

REVERED ONE, YOU ARE MUCH TOO FOND OF THE PANDAVAS. YOU DO NOT WANT THEM DEFEATED.

DURYODHANA, EVEN THE GODS CANNOT DEFEAT THE FORCES LED BY ARJUNA.

HOWEVER, TODAY I WILL SLAY AT LEAST ONE OF THE FOREMOST OF THE PANDAVA ARMY. BUT YOU MUST KEEP ARJUNA BUSY.

I WILL ASK THE SAMSHAPTAKAS* TO DRAW ARJUNA AWAY FROM THE THICK OF THE BATTLE.

SO ON THE THIRTEENTH DAY OF THE BATTLE, THE SAMSHAPTAKAS GREETED ARJUNA WITH WAR CRIES.

COME ON, ARJUNA! WE CHALLENGE YOU TO FIGHT WITH US!

ALL RIGHT, HERE I COME!

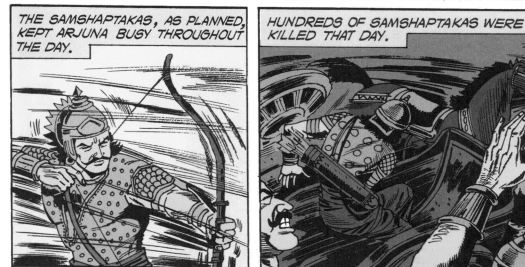

THE SAMSHAPTAKAS, AS PLANNED, KEPT ARJUNA BUSY THROUGHOUT THE DAY.

HUNDREDS OF SAMSHAPTAKAS WERE KILLED THAT DAY.

* A COMMUNITY OF SOLDIERS SWORN TO CONQUER OR DIE

AS NIGHT FELL, BOTH SIDES RETIRED TO THEIR CAMPS. ALTHOUGH HE WAS VICTORIOUS, ARJUNA WAS NOT HAPPY.

KRISHNA, I FEEL UNEASY. SOME UNKNOWN FEAR HAS SEIZED ME. I HOPE ALL IS WELL WITH MY BROTHERS.

DON'T WORRY, ARJUNA. NOT ONE OF THE KAURAVAS CAN EQUAL THEM IN STRENGTH OR VALOUR.

SOON THEY REACHED THEIR CAMP—

I DON'T HEAR THE LAUGHTER OF OUR MEN. AND WHERE IS MY SON, ABHIMANYU? WHY ISN'T HE HERE TO GREET ME?

WHEN HE ENTERED THE TENT, HE SAW HIS BROTHERS SITTING ALL CHEERLESS, PLUNGED IN GRIEF.

WHAT'S WRONG? WHERE IS ABHIMANYU?

BUT NO ONE REPLIED.

DRONA USED THE CHAKRAVYOOHA BATTLE FORMATION TODAY. YOU DIDN'T ASK ABHIMANYU TO PENETRATE IT, DID YOU?

WE DID, ARJUNA. WE HAD TO!

HE FOUGHT VALIANTLY...AND DIED A HERO'S DEATH!

DEAD! MY SON'S DEAD!

PERHAPS, MY SON, YOU THOUGHT THAT I WOULD COME TO YOUR RESCUE. I FAILED YOU!

ANGRILY, ARJUNA TURNED UPON HIS BROTHERS.

YOU WERE ON YOUR CHARIOTS. YOU WERE FULLY ARMED. WHY DIDN'T YOU PROTECT MY SON? YOU ARE ALL COWARDS!

ARJUNA, WE COULD NOT FOLLOW ABHIMANYU INTO THE CHAKRAVYOOHA. JAYADRATHA HELD US BACK. WE COULD NOT GET PAST HIM.

JAYADRATHA!

THEN ARJUNA TOOK A TERRIBLE VOW.

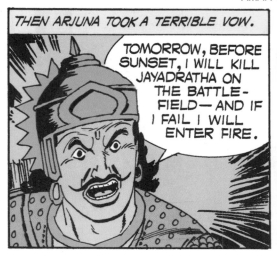

TOMORROW, BEFORE SUNSET, I WILL KILL JAYADRATHA ON THE BATTLE-FIELD— AND IF I FAIL I WILL ENTER FIRE.

ARJUNA AND KRISHNA BLEW THEIR CONCH-SHELLS LOUDLY...

... SENDING A WAVE OF FEAR INTO THE ENEMY'S CAMP.

WHAT AN EAR-PIERCING SOUND THAT IS!

BUT WHY ARE THEY BLOWING THEIR CONCHES NOW?

JUST THEN JAYADRATHA TOTTERED IN.

DURYODHANA, MY LIFE IS IN DANGER!

WHY? WHAT HAS HAPPENED?

16

JAYADRATHA TOLD HIM OF ARJUNA'S VOW—

SO ARJUNA WILL KILL HIMSELF IF HE FAILS TO KILL YOU BY SUNSET? EXCELLENT! WE HAVE ONLY TO PROTECT YOU UNTIL SUNSET AND YOU WILL BE SAFE.

JAYADRATHA FELT REASSURED.

I'VE BEEN FOOLISH. YOU CAN PROTECT A MAN FROM THE LORD OF DEATH HIMSELF. I DON'T HAVE TO FEAR ARJUNA.

MY ENTIRE ARMY WILL PROTECT YOU. AND AS FOR ARJUNA, YOU WILL SEE HIM ENTERING THE FIRE.

THE NEXT DAY DRONA MADE CAREFUL PREPARATIONS.

JAYADRATHA, YOU ARE IN NO DANGER. BETWEEN YOU AND ARJUNA STANDS OUR MASSIVE ARMY WHICH STRETCHES FOR OVER TWELVE MILES.

NOW I FEEL AT EASE.

DRONA TOOK HIS POSITION AT THE HEAD OF HIS ARMY. ARJUNA ARRIVED AT THE BATTLEFIELD WITH A HUGE ARMY AND SALUTED DRONA.

MASTER, BLESS ME. YOU TRAINED ME IN WARFARE. THROUGH YOUR GRACE, I WISH TO SLAY JAYADRATHA IN THE BATTLE.

WE ARE ON OPPOSING SIDES, ARJUNA. YOU MUST VANQUISH ME FIRST BEFORE YOU CAN REACH, JAYADRATHA.

GREAT WAS THE BATTLE THAT WAS FOUGHT BETWEEN MASTER AND PUPIL.

FINALLY—

ARJUNA, DRONA WILL KEEP US HERE THE WHOLE DAY. WE MUST SLIP PAST HIM SOMEHOW.

AS KRISHNA SKILFULLY DROVE THE CHARIOT FORWARD, DRONA CALLED OUT—

ARE YOU RUNNING AWAY FROM YOUR FOE?

YOU ARE MY TEACHER— NOT MY FOE. AND NO ONE CAN DEFEAT YOU IN BATTLE.

ARJUNA RELEASED A VOLLEY OF ARROWS TO CLEAR THE WAY. THEN HE CHARGED FORWARD LEAVING HIS ARMY FAR BEHIND.

RUN! ARJUNA IS HERE!

HERE COMES ARJUNA!

KING SHRUTAYUDHA, AN ALLY OF DURYODHANA, STOOD IN HIS WAY.

ARJUNA, YOU WON'T GET PAST ME!

AND YOU, KRISHNA, ARE THE POWER BEHIND ARJUNA. I WILL KILL YOU, TOO.

A FIERCE BATTLE ENSUED.

LORD VARUNA'S BOON HAS MADE HIM POWERFUL.

IS THERE NO WAY OF DEFEATING HIM?

ONLY ONE PERSON CAN BRING ABOUT HIS DEATH— SHRUTA-YUDHA HIMSELF.

HOW?

JUST THEN—

KRISHNA! WATCH OUT!

BUT KRISHNA SMILINGLY RECEIVED THE MACE ON HIS SHOULDER.

KRISHNA!

TO ARJUNA'S AMAZEMENT, KRISHNA WAS UNHURT—

OH! THE MACE HAS BOUNCED BACK!

JUST AS I HAD EXPECTED! LORD VARUNA HAD WARNED HIM THE MACE WOULD RECOIL ON HIMSELF, IF USED AGAINST SOMEONE WHO WAS UNARMED.

SHRUTAYUDHA REMEMBERED VARUNA'S WARNING. BUT IT WAS TOO LATE.

NO!

SHRUTAYUDHA FELL.

ARJUNA, THE UNDESERVING WHO OBTAIN POWER TO DESTROY OTHERS, FALL VICTIM TO THIS SAME POWER.

THE FALL OF SHRUTAYUDHA CAUSED PANIC IN DURYODHANA'S CAMP. JAYADRATHA WAS ALARMED AT THE NEWS.

DURYODHANA, IS THERE NO ONE WHO CAN HOLD ARJUNA BACK? HE WILL BE HERE SOON!

HE SHALL BE STOPPED.

URGED BY DURYODHANA, HUNDREDS OF WARRIORS FELL UPON ARJUNA.

THEN THE MIGHTY WARRIOR, SHRUTAYU, HURLED HIS SPEAR AT ARJUNA.

TAKE THIS, O ARJUNA!

THE SPEAR FOUND ITS MARK. STAGGERING UNDER THE IMPACT...

...ARJUNA SUPPORTED HIMSELF AGAINST HIS FLAGSTAFF.

A SHOUT OF JOY RENT THE AIR.

ARJUNA IS DEAD!

ARJUNA HAS BEEN KILLED!

BUT SOON ARJUNA RECOVERED AND INVOKED INTO EXISTENCE THE WEAPON NAMED AFTER INDRA, AND FROM IT FLOWED THOUSANDS OF ARROWS.

SHRUTAYU FELL AND HIS SOLDIERS BEGAN TO FLEE. ARJUNA'S CHARIOT SPED ON.

FASTER, KRISHNA, WE HAVE A LONG WAY TO GO BEFORE WE REACH JAYADRATHA.

BUT ANOTHER SECTION OF DURYODHANA'S ARMY BLOCKED HIS PATH.

FASTER, KRISHNA, FASTER.

OUR HORSES ARE TIRED AND THEY ARE PIERCED WITH ARROWS. WE CAN'T GO FASTER.

THEN LET'S UNHARNESS THE HORSES AND REMOVE THE ARROWS.

ARJUNA JUMPED DOWN FROM THE CHARIOT...

ARJUNA HAS DISMOUNTED!

...AND SHIELDED KRISHNA WITH A SHOWER OF ARROWS.

ARJUNA, OUR HORSES NEED WATER TO DRINK...

...BUT WHERE, ON A BATTLE-FIELD, CAN WE EXPECT TO FIND WATER?

HERE!

ARJUNA SHOT AN ARROW INTO THE GROUND...

...AND WATER GUSHED OUT, MAKING A POOL FOR THE HORSES TO DRINK FROM.

MEANWHILE, DURYODHANA'S MEN MADE A DETERMINED ATTACK —

NOW IS THE TIME TO OVERPOWER ARJUNA.

KILL HIM — AND HIS HORSES!

ARJUNA SWIFTLY CREATED A PROTECTIVE WALL OF ARROWS AROUND THE POOL.

KRISHNA TENDED THE HORSES...

... AND LOVINGLY MASSAGED THEM.

WHEN THE HORSES WERE REFRESHED, THEY WERE HARNESSED AGAIN AND KRISHNA AND ARJUNA SPEEDILY DROVE ON.

LOOK! KRISHNA AND ARJUNA ARE HERE AGAIN!

AND OUR ARROWS HAVE MADE NOT A SCRATCH ON THEM!

MEANWHILE JAYADRATHA WAS WATCHING THE SKY INTENTLY—

GOOD! JUST ONE MORE HOUR FOR THE SUN TO SET!

THEN ARJUNA, HAVING FAILED IN HIS MISSION, WILL PUT AN END TO HIS LIFE.

JUST THEN—

ARJUNA IS COMING!

DURYODHANA, PROTECT ME!

BE CALM, JAYADRATHA. I WILL GO AFTER HIM MYSELF.

WILL HE STOP ARJUNA? THIS ONE HOUR BEFORE THE SUN SETS WILL SEEM LIKE ETERNITY!

SOON DURYODHANA MET ARJUNA.

NO, ARJUNA. YOU CAN'T GET PAST ME. YOU CANNOT HARM JAYADRATHA.

JAYADRATHA SHALL DIE BEFORE THE SUN SETS TODAY.

ARJUNA SHATTERED DURYODHANA'S CHARIOT.

DURYODHANA'S MEN RUSHED TO HIS RESCUE.

DON'T ALLOW HIM TO GO AHEAD!

DURYODHANA'S MEN SURROUNDED ARJUNA'S CHARIOT.

ARJUNA, TIME IS RUNNING OUT. GET THEM OUT OF THE WAY.

WATCH ME, KRISHNA!

ARJUNA DREW HIS BOW, WHILE KRISHNA BLEW HIS CONCH.

THE BLARE OF KRISHNA'S CONCH AND THE TWANG OF ARJUNA'S BOW HAD A STUNNING EFFECT AND ALL OF DURYODHANA'S MEN FELL TO THE GROUND.

BEFORE THEY COULD RECOVER FROM THE SHOCK, KRISHNA SPURRED ON HIS HORSES.

AS THE EVENING SHADOWS LENGTHENED, THE PANDAVAS BECAME MORE AND MORE ANXIOUS...

WILL ARJUNA REACH JAYADRATHA IN TIME?

...AND THE KAURAVAS, MORE AND MORE JUBILANT.

SOON THE SUN WILL GO DOWN AND ARJUNA IS STILL FAR AWAY FROM JAYADRATHA!

BUT KEEP A CAREFUL WATCH. HE MUST BE KEPT AWAY FROM JAYADRATHA AT ALL COSTS.

URGED BY DURYODHANA, KARNA AND THE OTHER WARRIORS ATTACKED ARJUNA.

BUT THEY COULD NOT HOLD HIM OFF FOR LONG—

ARJUNA, AT LAST WE HAVE FOUND JAYADRATHA! THERE HE IS!

BUT, KRISHNA, THERE ARE SIX WARRIORS BETWEEN HIM AND ME. I WON'T BE ABLE TO KILL JAYADRATHA BEFORE THE SUN SETS!

NO, YOU SHALL SLAY HIM!

SUDDENLY IT BECAME DARK.

KRISHNA! THE SUN HAS SET!

NO, ARJUNA. THIS IS AN ILLUSION. YOU HAVE NOTHING TO FEAR.

JAYADRATHA AND HIS FRIENDS WERE DECEIVED BY THE ILLUSION OF DARKNESS CAUSED BY KRISHNA.

DARKNESS AT LAST! I AM SAFE!

DURYODHANA'S MEN PUT DOWN THEIR WEAPONS AND STOOD UP TO CHEER THE JUBILANT JAYADRATHA.

ARJUNA WILL NOW PUT AN END TO HIS LIFE!

DIDN'T I TELL YOU WE WOULD PROTECT YOU?

THEN ARJUNA STRUCK—

AT THAT MOMENT THE DARKNESS WAS DISPELLED AND THE SUN WAS VISIBLE AGAIN.

THE SUN HAS NOT SET! IT WAS ONLY AN ILLUSION WROUGHT BY KRISHNA!

I HAVE FAILED YOU, JAYADRATHA!

VICTORIOUS, KRISHNA AND ARJUNA BLEW THEIR CONCHES TO ANNOUNCE THEIR VICTORY.

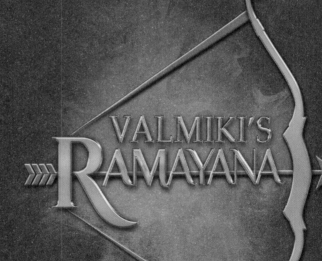